MAGIC FOREST

FUTURE

MYSTERY ISLAND

DOJANG

OCEAN

SUBWAY

FAVORITE BAKERY

SUBWAY

THE TRAIN HOME

Dan-ah Kim

GREENWILLOW BOOKS

An Imprint of HarperCollinsPublishers

For my family, near and far

The Train Home
Copyright © 2023 by Danah Kim
All rights reserved. Manufactured in Italy.
For information address HarperCollins Children's Books,
a division of HarperCollins Publishers, 195 Broadway, New York, NY 10007.
www.harpercollinschildrens.com

The artwork was created with mixed media (gouache, acrylic, pencil,
colored pencil, cut paper, thread) and edited in Adobe Photoshop®.
The text type is 20-point Maxime.

Library of Congress Cataloging-in-Publication Data is available.

ISBN 9780063076914 (hardcover)
23 24 25 26 27 RTLO 10 9 8 7 6 5 4 3 2 1
First Edition

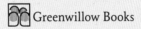 Greenwillow Books

Nari lives in a rowdy home in a crowded city.
Sometimes it feels a bit too full
and a little too loud for Nari,
and she wishes she lived somewhere else.

Somewhere with a flower garden
and a clear view of the night sky.

A room full of books.

Maybe by the ocean?

Or in the middle
of the woods,
like she's seen
in pictures.

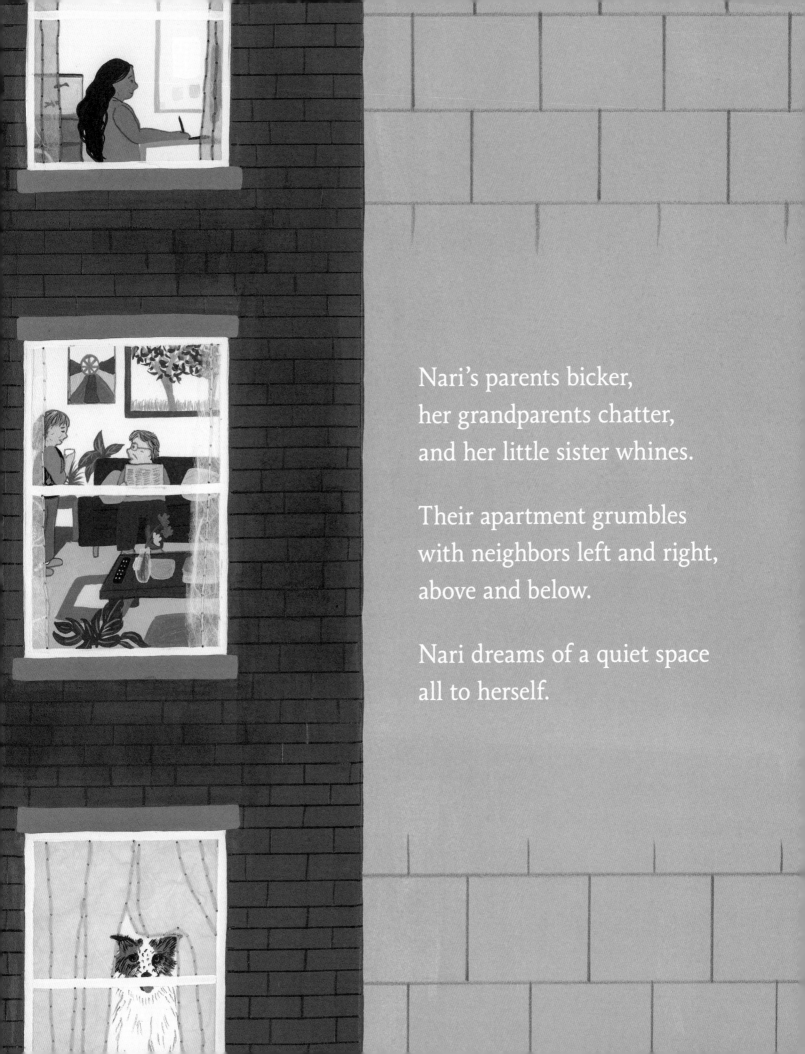

Nari's parents bicker,
her grandparents chatter,
and her little sister whines.

Their apartment grumbles
with neighbors left and right,
above and below.

Nari dreams of a quiet space
all to herself.

The train rumbles by
outside her window.

Maybe Nari can take it . . .

to find her *dream* home.

In the woods, Nari would build a big nest where she could sleep and dream in the treetops.

But where else
can the train take her?

The next stop smells of salty sea air.

Could the train take her under the waves?

She'd live by a delicate
coral reef, with the
brightest neighbors.

Or maybe on top of the water, in a peaceful houseboat.

She would sway with the waves and watch the stars.

But before
she floats
away . . .

Nari can take the train to a massive room
full of books and guarded by lions.

She might find a story
that reminds her of her grandparents,
full of bravery and adventure.

The train can even take her backward in time.
Next time, she should bring her sister,
who can name each lost animal and dinosaur.

Or the train can take Nari to live in the sky,
with her favorite constellation.
She makes a wish on the brightest star
that her parents were there to share the view.

Everything is beautiful.

But in the quiet,
she misses her parents' laughter,
her grandparents' stories,
and her sister's singing.

Nari follows comets back down to Earth.

The train can take her to the homes of animals, flowers, books, and stars.

But she knows where she will go next.

Nari will go where her favorite people in the world are gathered.

Where she can listen to their songs and stories.

She will take the train home.